CLEO'S ALPHABET BOOK

Caroline Mockford

Barefoot Books
Celebrating Art and Story

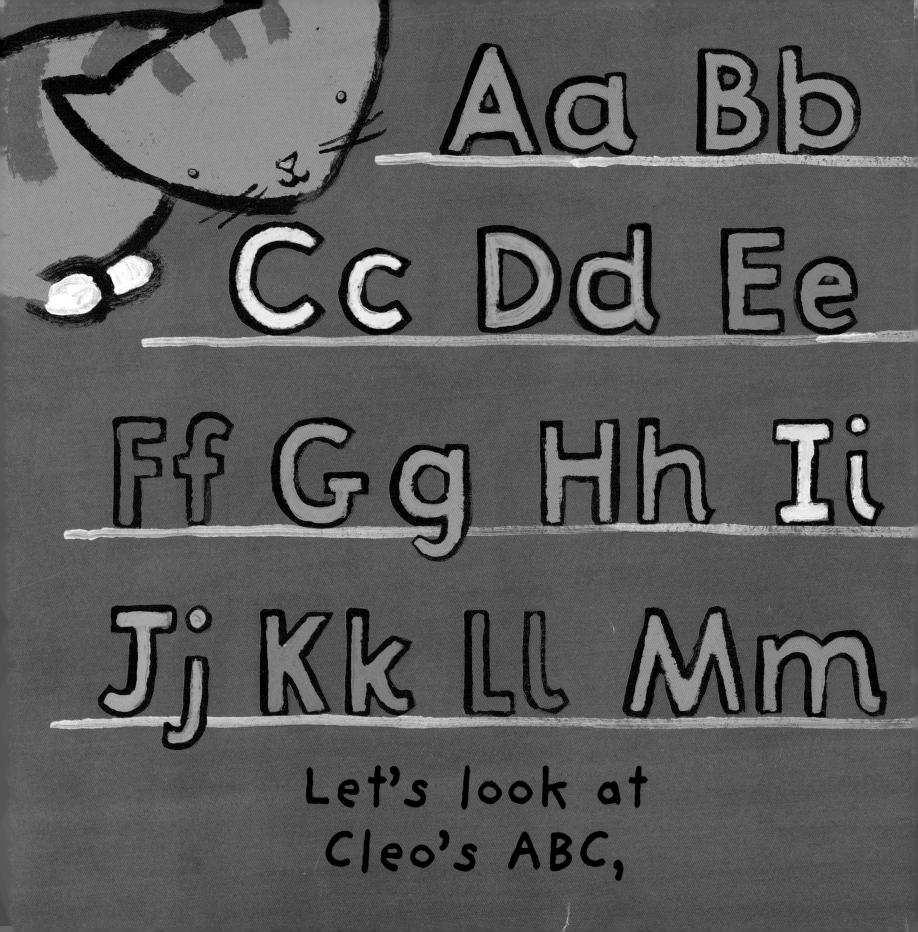

Aa Bb
Cc Dd Ee
Ff Gg Hh Ii
Jj Kk Ll Mm

Let's look at
Cleo's ABC,

Nn Oo Pp

Qq Rr Ss Tt

Uu Vv Ww

Xx Yy Zz

and guess what all
the words will be!

Aa

A is crunchy, crisp and red.

B floats on the waves.

C moos
when she says hello.

D d

D barks as he plays.

Ee

E is good for us to eat.

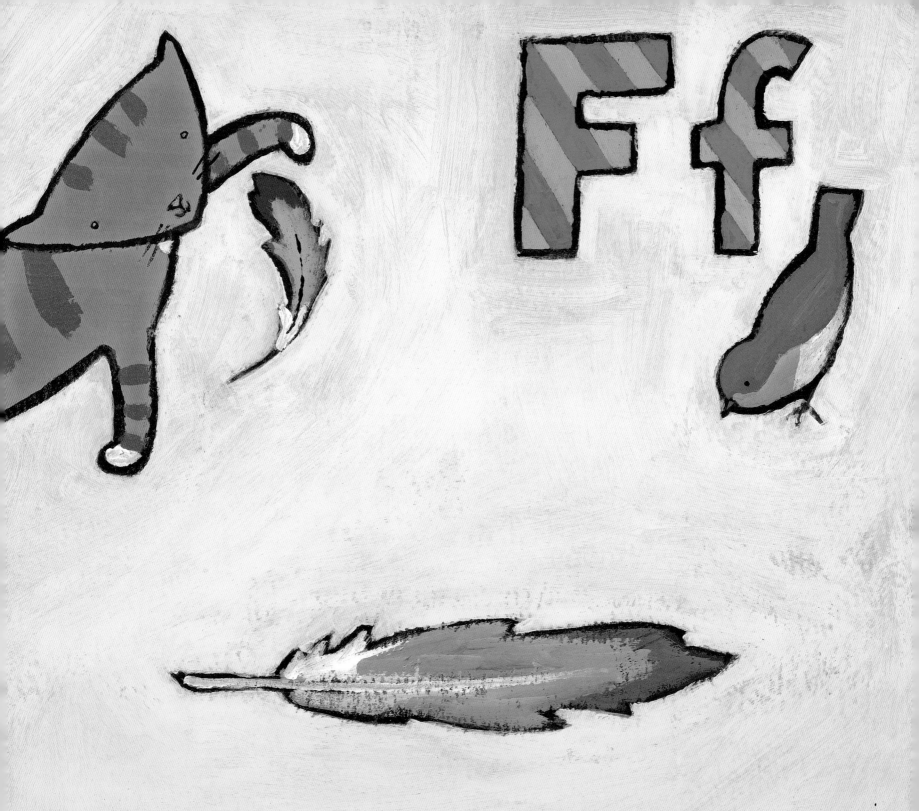

F is what birds wear.

Gg

G makes people's
hands feel warm.

H sits on their hair.

I i

I is round
and made of ice.

J makes toast taste sweet.

K k

K loves
dancing in the wind.

L lights up the street.

M is Cleo's favorite drink.

N is home for birds.

O is juicy, sweet and round.

P makes shapes and words.

Q keeps Cleo
warm and snug.

R r

R climbs up the wall.

S shines brightly
in the night.

T grows green and tall.

U protects us from the rain.

V drives far away.

Ww

W turns round and round.

X is fun to play.

Y y

Y means Cleo's sleepy now.
Z means time to rest.

Let's practice Cleo's ABC and all the words we've guessed!

For my mother — S. B.
For Sonny — C. M.

Barefoot Books
2067 Massachusetts Ave, 5th Floor
Cambridge, MA 02140

This book is printed on 100% acid-free paper
The illustrations were prepared in acrylics on 140lb watercolor paper
Design by Jennie Hoare, England
Typeset in 44 pt Providence Sans bold
Color separation by Bright Arts Graphics, Singapore
Printed and bound in Singapore by Tien Wah Press (Pte.) Ltd.

1 3 5 7 9 8 6 4 2

Publisher Cataloging-in-Publication Data (U.S.)

Blackstone, Stella.
  Cleo's alphabet book / [Stella Blackstone] ; Caroline Mockford. —1st ed.
[32] p. : col. ill. ;   cm.
Note: "Text copyright © 2003 by Stella Blackstone" — copyright page.
Summary: Cleo the cat introduces children to the alphabet, asking children to
guess words based upon their first letter as well as clues in the text and art.
ISBN 1-84148-008-8
1. Alphabet books. 2. Cats — Fiction. 1. Mockford, Caroline. 11. Title.
[E] 21   PZ8.3B534Ca 2003

Barefoot Books
Celebrating Art and Story

At Barefoot Books, we celebrate art and story with books that open the hearts and minds of children from all walks of life, inspiring them to read deeper, search further, and explore their own creative gifts. Taking our inspiration from many different cultures, we focus on themes that encourage independence of spirit, enthusiasm for learning, and acceptance of other traditions. Thoughtfully prepared by writers, artists, and storytellers from all over the world, our products combine the best of the present with the best of the past to educate our children as the caretakers of tomorrow.

www.barefootbooks.com

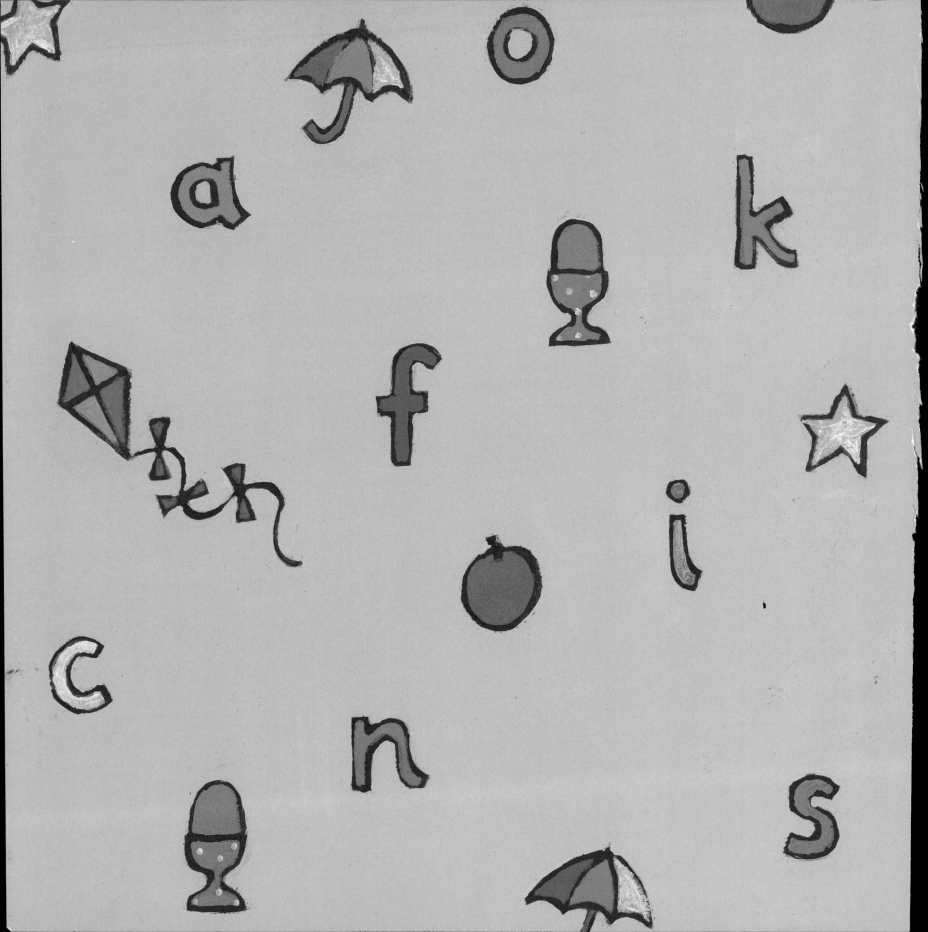